Disney's
Winnie the Pooh
Giving Is the Best Gift

Gifts are always great to get,

From friends both kind and true.

But giving's even better yet.

Here's something just for you!

A bear named Pooh sat at his breakfast table, licking the last bit of honey from his hands. His tummy was pleasantly full, and his mind started to wander.

He hummed a dum-de-dum-de-diddle song as he looked around his house.

Pooh saw all kinds of wonderful things that his friends had given him over the years. There were the red mittens that Kanga had knitted for him; a bright blue kite from Roo; a pogo stick from Tigger; and a sailboat from Piglet.

"Perhaps," thought Pooh, "I should do something nice for my friends today."

He decided he would give them each a present to show how much he enjoyed their friendship. Pooh wouldn't even tell them the presents were from him—it would be a secret!

Pooh realized that another pair of hands would come in handy f
his plan. So he asked Christopher Robin for some help.
"After all," said Pooh, "giving is the best gift of all."

"I want to write each person a poem to go with the present," Pooh explained. "But I don't want anyone to know it's from me."

"Then we'll simply sign each one 'From Your Secret Friend'" said Christopher Robin.

Kanga was the first to receive a gift. She found a beautiful package in her mailbox with a little note:

Because you're always nice and sweet,
Here's a present for you to eat.
It's sticky and yummy and yellow, too.
And best of all, it's just for you!

Kanga carefully untied the bow and opened the box.
Inside it was a little pot of honey.

"Oh!" she thought to herself. "What a sweet gift from
Roo! He always loves to bake honey cake with me."

Next, Tigger discovered a package with a note for him:
To Tigger, it read, *Because you're always the best,*
Here's something to help you stand out from the rest.
It has lots of stripes—in orange, not blue,
And best of all, it's just for you!

Tigger quickly ripped off the wrapping paper and found an orange-striped scarf.

"Hoo-hoo-hoo!" he exclaimed, tying it around his neck. "Whaddaya know? A secret pal brought me a present! It must be from my little buddy Piglet."

From behind a tree, Pooh and Christopher Robin watched
Tigger bouncing around in his new scarf.

"It's working," whispered Pooh. "No one suspects that I'm
the 'secret friend'"!

While Kanga and Roo were busy playing outside, Christopher Robin kept watch as Pooh sneaked into their house.

He left some pretty colored kite ribbons under Roo's pillow with a note, then tiptoed quietly back outside.

"Hey, what's this?" asked Roo when he went inside for a nap.
Pooh listened outside his window as Christopher Robin read the no

Roo, you know that we always have fun,
Just strolling around any day in the sun.
To thank you, I'm leaving this little surprise,
A ribbon to tie to your kite when it flies.

"Oh, this must be from Mama!" Roo said happily to Christopher Robin. "We always have so much fun playing outside together."

Then he drifted off to sleep.

Later, Pooh spied Piglet skipping down a quiet path.

"I'll keep him busy," said Christopher Robin. "You run ahead and leave the present."

Christopher Robin stopped to chat with Piglet while Pooh placed the package just a few steps in front of the path.

Piglet turned back to the path and was surprised to see a tiny, red polka-dotted box with a gold bow on it.

"Oh, my! What's this?" he asked Christopher Robin.

Christopher Robin read the note inside for Piglet:
Friends are for sharing adventures and such,
That's why we're always together so much!
This lucky coin will bring you good cheer,
And help you remember I'll always be here!

"Oh, my!" exclaimed Piglet. "That Tigger is always full of surprises. What a wonderful present!"

And with that, Piglet picked up his lucky coin, said goodbye to Christopher Robin, and gleefully skipped along.

By now everyone was delighted with their gifts. And since Pooh's friends all thought they knew who the presents were from, they decided to get little gifts for their "secret friends" in return.

Soon everybody gathered in the middle of the Hundred-Acre Wood to exchange gifts. But when the presents were handed out, everyone looked a little confused.

No one would admit to being the "secret friend."
"But Mama, isn't it you?" asked Roo.
"No, I thought it was you, little Roo," said Kanga.
"Tigger, isn't this your surprise?" said Piglet.
"Not me, Buddy Boy!" insisted Tigger.

Just then everyone noticed that Pooh was being very quiet.
"Hmm, I got a funny feelin' about this," said Tigger. "This
gift-giving fella likes honey, flies kites, likes my stripes—"
"And is a friend to all of us!" said Piglet.

Pooh shrugged bashfully. "Oh, bother," he said, blushing.
Then everyone agreed all at once: "Pooh, it must be you!"

"Yes, it is," said Pooh. "But I wanted it to be a secret."

"That was such a nice thing to do, Pooh," said Piglet.

"Why wouldn't you tell us?"

"I didn't want you to know," explained Pooh. "Or to give me any gifts in return."

"But why not?" asked Tigger. "Presents are fun."

"I think I know," said Roo. "It's because giving is the best gift of all!"

A LESSON A DAY
POOH'S WAY

It's always *better*

to give a little

smackerel of something

than to receive.